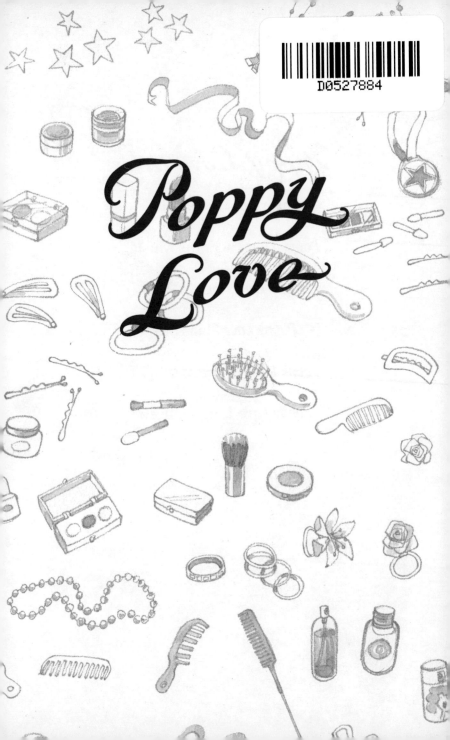

Poppy
Love

Poppy Love titles

Poppy Love
In the Spotlight

NATASHA MAY

illustrated by
SHELAGH MCNICHOLAS

WALKER
BOOKS

With thanks to Neil Kelly and the students of
Rubies Dance Centre
N.M.

With thanks to Carolyn, Julia, Kirsty and Ann at
Bell's Dance Centre
S.M.

First published 2009 by Walker Books Ltd
87 Vauxhall Walk, London SE11 5HJ

2 4 6 8 10 9 7 5 3 1

Text © 2009 Veronica Bennett
Illustrations © 2009 Shelagh McNicholas

This book has been typeset in ITC Giovanni

Printed and bound in Great Britain by Clays Ltd, St Ives plc

British Library Cataloguing in Publication Data:
a catalogue record for this book is available from the British Library

ISBN 978-1-4063-2011-4

www.walker.co.uk

Contents

Top Ten

Poppy Love loved ballroom dancing.

She and her partner, Zack Bishop, had dance lessons three times a week with Miss Johnson at the Blue Horizon Dance Studio. They had medals for passing exams, and had been successful in competitions, too. They had even qualified to take part in the Nationwide Finals to compete for the biggest prize of all – Nationwide Stardance Champion.

"How did you feel when *you* first danced in the Nationwide Finals, when you were a little girl?" Poppy asked her Auntie Jill, who used to be a champion ballroom dancer. "I mean, you have to know ten dances, but you don't know which ones you'll be doing until they tell you, just before you go on. Were you scared?"

Auntie Jill and Poppy were in Auntie Jill's brand-new kitchen in her brand-new house, having drinks at the brand-new breakfast bar. She considered Poppy's question. "Not quite *scared*," she said, stirring her coffee. "More like excited fit to burst! I used to get a pain in my stomach."

"I get that too," agreed Poppy. "But it goes away once I start dancing."

Auntie Jill nodded. "Exactly. And then afterwards I always felt like I could do all ten dances a hundred times and not get tired."

"Exactly!" said Poppy, and she and her aunt laughed.

"That reminds me, Poppy," said Auntie Jill, "I've got something to ask you."

Poppy stopped in the middle of sipping her orange juice. "What is it?" she asked.

"Well," said Auntie Jill, "now that Uncle Simon and I have moved into this new house…"

Poppy nodded. She couldn't speak because she was holding her breath, wondering if her aunt remembered a promise she'd once made. Auntie Jill had told her that if she ever moved to a house with a garden, she would get Poppy a puppy and keep it for her – you

couldn't keep a dog
in a flat at the top of a
hotel, which was where
the Love family lived.
Auntie Jill still worked
at the Hotel Gemini,
just like she'd always
done, but her new

house had a lovely garden with a large lawn.

"We thought we'd do something to
celebrate," said Auntie Jill. "You know, like a
house-warming party."

This didn't sound as if it would include a
puppy. Poppy tried not to feel disappointed.
"That would be fun," she said.

"I want to ask you about an idea I've got
for a dancing game," said Auntie Jill. "Do you
think you and your friends would help out?"

Poppy was interested. "What would we have to do?" she asked.

"Well, dance!" replied Auntie Jill, smiling. "I thought it might be fun to have a requests show, like they have on the radio, only with dances instead of songs."

It *did* sound fun. "How would it work?" asked Poppy.

"We'll make a list of all the dances you know, and give it to the party guests. They will then call out whichever dance they want to see, until you've done ten from the list. We could call the game Top Ten."

Poppy thought about the dances she knew. Apart from the ten required for competition, there were also Latin dances, like the salsa, the lambada and the meringue, as well as the rock 'n' roll from the 1950s and the twist from the 1960s. There seemed to be a lot!

"I hope we can remember them all!" she said.

"I'll help you practise," offered Auntie Jill. "Will you ask your friends? The party is in two weeks' time."

Poppy looked at her aunt's eager face. Auntie Jill loved dancing, and wanted her party guests to enjoy themselves too. Poppy knew that Zack and all her other ballroom-dancing friends would help.

"I'll see them at dance class on Wednesday," she said. "I'm sure they'd love to do it – they all love parties!"

Auntie Jill gave Poppy a hug. "Thanks, Poppy," she said happily.

The living-room in the new house had a woodblock floor. Auntie Jill and Uncle

Simon had taken away the rug and pushed the sofas against one wall. When Poppy, Zack and their friends arrived for the house-warming party, the dance floor was all ready for them.

"Look at this!" exclaimed Sam, his eyes wide. "There's loads of room!"

"It's like a ballroom!" added Zack.

"This is going to be fun!" said Sophie, Sam's partner.

Cora, looking very pretty in a pink dress with a pink ribbon in her curly dark hair, pulled Luke into the middle of the room. She sang a cha-cha-cha rhythm, and she and Luke began to dance.

"She just can't wait!" explained Luke.

Poppy felt very pleased that her friends were so enthusiastic about joining in Auntie Jill's game. Uncle Simon's nephew,

Little Tom, had only been going to dance classes for a short while, but he and his partner, Emma, refused to be left out. "I already know most of the dances," Little Tom had told Poppy, "and Emma and Auntie Jill will help too. Please, Poppy!"

Once he started practising the dances, Little Tom learnt fast. When he and Emma arrived, Poppy could see that he was more excited than any of the others about the Top Ten game.

He rushed in, almost skidding on the polished floor. "What have you done to this room?" he asked Uncle Simon. "It looks bigger."

"Well, we've pushed the walls back," Uncle Simon told him seriously.

"And made the ceiling higher. Just for tonight, though. We'll put it all back tomorrow."

Everyone laughed, even Little Tom, though Poppy wondered if, just for a moment, he'd believed their uncle's words.

"I think it's perfect," said Emma. "And this is a great idea for a party game."

Auntie Jill smiled at the children. "Let's get you some drinks," she said. "And I expect you could eat some party food too, couldn't you?"

"Yes, please!" said Sam, who loved to eat almost as much as he loved to dance.

Uncle Simon put the music on while Auntie Jill served drinks and put plates of food on the table. Soon the guests started to arrive and the party began.

Poppy's mum and dad and her brother, Tom, were there, and Zack's mum, and Poppy's friends' parents and brothers and sisters. Auntie Jill had invited some of her own friends from the dance world, and people who worked at Uncle Simon's restaurant and the Hotel Gemini were there too. Lots of them brought their children. The living-room soon filled with chatter and laughter and chinking glasses – the sound of people enjoying themselves.

"See," said Little Tom to Poppy, biting into a doughnut, "we *do* know loads of people. I bet I'll do something wrong and they'll laugh."

"Well, I bet you won't," said Poppy. She looked at her cousin carefully. "You'd better get that jam off your mouth, though, or they *will* laugh!"

Auntie Jill was giving out pieces of paper to the guests.  "You can request any dance you like, and I guarantee you'll see it performed," she explained. "Beautifully, of course!" she added, catching Poppy's eye as she passed.

On the paper was a list of eighteen dances. Poppy and Zack stared at it.

"I can't believe we know *eighteen* dances," said Zack.

"Neither can I," said Poppy. "Thank goodness we're only doing ten, though we don't know which ten!"

The party guests applauded as the children walked out onto the floor. Cora in her pink dress and Luke in black trousers and a pink shirt led the way, followed by Emma, looking sunshiny in yellow, with her fair hair in a swingy pony tail, and Little Tom walking proudly beside her in his yellow shirt. Then came Sophie and Sam in turquoise, both smiling widely, and then Poppy and Zack. Poppy wore her dress that was the colour of mint ice cream, and Zack had a shirt to match.

"You all look terrific!" called a voice Poppy recognized. It was Dad, giving them a thumbs-up from the back of the audience.

Simon stood by the CD player. "Let's play Top Ten!" he announced. "Who's first?"

Mrs Feltham, Emma's mum, put up her hand. "The samba would be a good one to start with," she suggested, and everyone clapped. Simon played the samba music, the children prepared, and when the right beat came, off they went.

Poppy didn't feel nervous at all. It was just like dancing in her bedroom at home, or at dance class. The people watching weren't testing or judging her and her friends. Everyone was simply having fun. She and Zack twirled and swayed and rolled their hips to the lively Brazilian music, and Poppy, Cora and Sophie did the cartwheels from a samba show-dance routine they'd performed in the summer. The party guests whooped and clapped.

When the music ended, almost before the children could get their breath back, someone called, "Viennese waltz!"

In the Viennese waltz you had to spin. Round and round went the couples, first one way, then the other, the boys leading their partners in the correct ballroom hold, round and round the floor. It was a romantic dance, done to beautiful old-fashioned waltz music. But the music was quite fast and didn't give the children much time to rest after the samba.

Auntie Jill noticed this. "We'll have a five minute break before the next request!" she called. "Top up your drinks, folks, and help yourselves to food!"

"Thanks, Mrs Forrester," said Luke.

Auntie Jill smiled as she handed him a drink. "It's supposed to be fun," she said. "It's not meant to wear you out!"

"It *is* fun!" said Luke and Sam and Sophie and Zack together.

"I wonder what we'll get next?" added Emma. "I hope it's the paso doble. That's my favourite."

It wasn't the paso doble. In fact, it wasn't one of the main competition dances. With a big grin, a boy about Poppy's brother's age requested the rock 'n' roll. This was one of the club dances, done just for fun. The four couples threw themselves into the push-pull steps, the twists, turns and tricks of the rock 'n' roll, the audience clapping and tapping their feet in time to the beat. Poppy felt breathless, but happy. This was going well!

"All of you can join in that one later," said Uncle Simon when the rock 'n' roll was over. "Now, what's next?"

"The tango!" called someone.

"No, the foxtrot!" called someone else.

"I'd like to see the merengue," suggested another guest. "Or perhaps the quickstep?"

"One at a time!" laughed Uncle Simon.

The game was so successful that Poppy and her friends ended up dancing not ten, but *twelve* out of the eighteen dances! They had no time to practise between dances, or rehearse moves. They just had to dance what people requested straight away. The guests were amazed. When the game finished, they gathered round the children.

"How do you remember all the steps?" asked a man Poppy hadn't seen before.

"I don't know," answered Poppy. It was true. She didn't know how she remembered them, she just did. "Maybe we just practise them so much, we don't get time to forget them."

"And such lovely dresses and handsome partners!" said the man's wife.

Poppy recognized her – she worked at Uncle Simon's restaurant, showing people to their tables and bringing them drinks. "I might take up ballroom dancing myself!" she added.

"That was fantastic!" Auntie Jill said to the children. Poppy could tell by her shining eyes how pleased she was that the party was going so well. "Doing a dance without warning doesn't seem so hard now, does it, Poppy?"

Poppy looked at Zack, realizing what her aunt's words meant. At the same moment,

Sophie, Sam, Cora and Luke – who were all going to compete in the Nationwide Finals – realized too. There was a silence.

Poppy was the first to speak. "So it was a game ... but was it also to help us practise?"

"No, of course not," said Uncle Simon, even though the children could see he was joking. He put his arm around his wife's shoulders. "Pretty clever idea, wasn't it?"

The children agreed. "And the best bit," said Sam when everyone else had stopped talking, "was that it didn't feel like practising at all. It was just fun!"

"Great," said Auntie Jill. "That's just what dancing *should* be."

Ugly Sisters

Christmas was only a few weeks away. Poppy had been so busy lately that she hadn't even thought about it. But one morning at school, all that changed.

Mr Quayle, Poppy's teacher, sat down at the piano. "This year," he said to the children, "the Linden Tree Junior School Christmas pantomime is ..." He held up some sheet music. "... *Cinderella!*"

The boys groaned and the girls cheered.
"Can I be Cinderella, sir?" called out Ryan
Buxton, a boy who was always sneering at
Poppy's dancing. "Since I'm so bee-oo-ti-ful?"

"Actually, Ryan," said Mr Quayle when the
class had stopped laughing, "I do have a part
in mind for you. I think you'd be very good
as one of the ugly sisters."

The thought of Ryan Buxton in the costume
of a pantomime ugly sister was so funny that
everyone began to laugh again.

"Of course, Cinderella has *two* ugly sisters,"
continued Mr Quayle. "Marc Jackson will be
playing the other one. All right, Marc?"

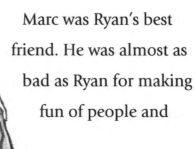

Marc was Ryan's best
friend. He was almost as
bad as Ryan for making
fun of people and

being mean, although Poppy knew he was
OK when he was on his own.

"No, sir, not me!" complained Marc,
pulling his jumper over his head.

"What's wrong?" asked Mr Quayle. "You
and Ryan would like to clown around on
stage, wouldn't you? Just like you do in the
classroom? And sing and dance too?"

Marc poked his head out of his jumper
and stared at Mr Quayle, and everyone else
groaned. They could imagine Ryan and Marc
clowning, but *dancing*?

"Yes, dance," said Mr Quayle firmly. "Now,
who knows what a choreographer is?"

Poppy put her hand up straight away.
"Someone who makes up the steps for
dances," she said, "and shows the dancers
how to do them."

"That's your job then, Poppy Love," said Mr Quayle. His eyes gleamed mischievously. "And everyone – *especially* Ryan and Marc – will have to do as you say."

Like all the other girls, Poppy had been hoping she would get the part of Cinderella. But being the choreographer sounded just as exciting. "Yes, sir!" she said.

Mr Quayle played some chords on the piano, and they began to learn a song from the pantomime. Poppy's friend Mia Porter sang so well that she was chosen as Cinderella. Poppy was delighted for her. Even when they were back in the classroom doing maths, the two girls couldn't stop talking about the pantomime.

"I'm nervous already!" said Mia, squirming in her seat.

"My auntie says it's good to be a bit nervous before a performance," replied Poppy. "It makes you do it better."

"I hope she's right," said Mia.

Poppy sharpened her pencil, thinking about the pantomime. As well as being the choreographer, she was going to be one of the six white mice that turned into ponies and pulled Cinderella's coach. Her face would be covered by a mask, so the audience wouldn't even know who she was. She hoped that all her family, especially Dad, whose job in London kept him so busy, would still come and see her – even if they couldn't *recognize* her!

She also had to teach Marc and Ryan their steps, and show twelve other children how to do a waltz for the ballroom scene. On top of all that, she had to learn her own dances for Miss Johnson's Christmas show, which was on the first Saturday of the holidays. Thinking about it all gave her a tight feeling in her stomach.

Poppy began the next sum, trying to put everything except maths out of her mind. But she knew what she had told Mia was true. If you didn't feel a bit nervous, you didn't dance so well.

The children quickly learned the steps of the waltz. In fact, they enjoyed the dancing so much that Poppy's main problem was making sure none of them fell off the stage as they whirled around!

But when Poppy tried to show Ryan Buxton and Marc Jackson what to do, they wouldn't listen.

"Why have we got to dance with each other?" asked Marc. "It's weird."

"It's not *weird*," insisted Poppy. "It's to make people laugh, that's all."

The ugly sisters had to do a song and dance to cha-cha-cha music, which would look very funny. But no one would be laughing if the boys refused to dance at all.

"Come on," said Poppy, trying to stay cheerful, "you've learnt the song, haven't you?"

The song was called "Two Lovely Wallflowers". The ugly sisters, outraged because no one was asking them to dance, showed off at the ball by singing the song and doing the cha-cha-cha. Mr Quayle had given Poppy a CD of the music. "Make the dance as silly as you like," he'd told her.

"We're not singing in front of *you*!" Marc told Poppy.

Poppy sighed. "All right, then," she said, "let's just try some dance moves."

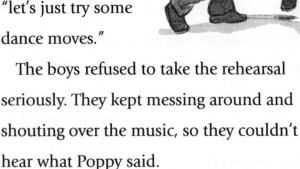

The boys refused to take the rehearsal seriously. They kept messing around and shouting over the music, so they couldn't hear what Poppy said.

In the end she turned the CD player off. "Look," she said, "just try the steps without the music. Stand behind me and follow what I do. There's only ten minutes left of lunchtime anyway."

Ryan and Marc exchanged a weary look. "Ten minutes of torture," said Marc, but he went and stood behind Poppy. "Come on, Ry," he said to his friend. "At least it'll give us a laugh."

Neither of the boys could do the steps very well, but Ryan was the clumsiest. He wouldn't stop sniggering and pushing Marc. And he refused to learn the routine.

"Which one's your left foot?" Poppy asked him.

"This one," said Ryan, holding up his right foot.

"Ryan!" Poppy knew he was doing it on purpose. "This isn't funny!"

Then the bell went and they had to stop.

"I don't feel like an ugly sister," said Marc, pulling on his school sweater. "I just feel like me, looking a right muppet in front of the whole school."

All afternoon, Poppy kept thinking about what Marc had said. If only she could make it easier for the boys to see that they were *playing* silly people, but weren't silly themselves. That way, they wouldn't mind the audience laughing at the song and dance.

In the evening, she stood in front of the big mirror in her bedroom, listening to the "Two Lovely Wallflowers" music and doing the cha-cha-cha steps. As she watched her short practice skirt flipping around her legs, she had an idea.

The ugly sisters' skirts would be long and full, with lots of petticoats. Under them, like

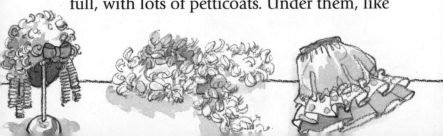

all pantomime dames, Ryan and Marc would have gaudy tights and pointed shoes.

They could use their costumes as part of the dance!

In a box at the bottom of the wardrobe was an old evening gown of Mum's that Poppy used to wear for dressing up when she was younger. The long velvet skirt had been shortened, but it still came down to Poppy's ankles, and stuck out all around. The moment she had it on, and was moving to the cha-cha-cha music again, she began to smile. It *did* look ridiculous, just like Mr Quayle wanted. She held out the skirt, swishing it around as she danced. She bumped her bottom against an imaginary partner's bottom, and laughed. "That's better!" she said to herself.

Poppy brought her long skirt to the next dress rehearsal, and Mr Quayle helped her find another one in the school costume basket. "Here," she said to the boys. "Put these on, please."

The boys grabbed the skirts and scrambled into them. They paraded around, thinking they looked side-splittingly funny. Shouting with laughter, they insulted each other and play-fought so much that half the rehearsal went by without any dancing at all.

Poppy was disappointed, and hungry because she hadn't had her lunch yet. She decided to try something else.

"All right," she said, "let's forget it. If you just want to muck about, I'll ask Mr Quayle to get two other boys to be the ugly sisters." She went down the steps from the stage. "You've missed your chance to be the stars of the pantomime. I'm going to get my lunch now."

But before she could leave the hall, Marc jumped off the stage and followed her. "But you can't walk out!" he shouted.

Poppy tried not to laugh. Marc's face was serious, but he was still wearing the long skirt.

"Why not?" she asked him. "Just watch me."

Ryan joined his friend. His skirt was too long for him, and he almost tripped several times as he crossed the hall. "But we'll get into trouble," he said.

"That's right," said Poppy calmly, "you will."

The three of them stood there looking at one another. Then Poppy said, "If you don't do this properly, you won't be doing it at all."

Marc glanced at Ryan, who shrugged.

"OK, Poppy," said Marc. "We might as well have a go, since we've been learning the lines, and the songs and everything."

"It's this stupid dancing," said Ryan moodily. "It's too hard."

"Not if you know which foot's which," said Poppy. "Now, which one's the left?"

This time he held up his left foot.

"Thank goodness!" she said. "You start on that one, OK?

They went back to the stage and Poppy stood in front of the boys. "After three," she said. "One, two, three, go!"

The boys began to do the cha-cha-cha steps, and Ryan even remembered to begin with his left foot. "One-and-two, and one-and-two," Poppy called out. "That's right. Now, turn-

and-*one* and turn-and-*two* and *keep going*!"

After two more attempts, Poppy put the music on and they did the routine without stopping. To her amazement, the boys whooped and slapped each other's hands. Ryan was so pleased with himself that he tripped over his skirt and almost fell on his face. But he didn't seem to mind.

"Come on," said Poppy, relieved. "Let's do it again."

The first performance of *Cinderella* came round very quickly. Before Poppy knew it, she was under the hot stage lights in her white leotard and tights and her mouse mask. When the lights went off, the mice changed their masks, and they appeared again as ponies when the lights went on again. Under her mask, Poppy smiled as the audience gasped.

Then it was the ballroom scene. Poppy watched anxiously, but no one did anything wrong in the waltz. The ugly sisters' cha-cha-cha was so funny that everyone roared with laughter. At the end of the scene Poppy heard someone clapping louder than everyone else.

It was Dad. She could see him sitting on the end of a row, smiling from ear to ear, and whispering to someone's dad on the other side of the aisle. She felt a bit embarrassed, but happy.

Ryan and Marc were the hit of the show. The audience stood and cheered

when they took their curtsey at the end, holding out their long skirts. Poppy clapped too, as hard as she could.

She was just getting into the car when Ryan crossed the car park with his parents. He waved to Poppy, and she waved back.

"See you tomorrow night!" he called to her.

"You too!" called Poppy.

"Who's that boy?" asked Mum as Dad started the car. "He seems very friendly."

"Ryan Buxton," said Poppy. "He played one of the ugly sisters."

It was dark in the car, so Poppy couldn't see Mum's face very well. But she could tell by the way Mum's head flicked round quickly that she was surprised. "Ryan Buxton?" she said. "That boy who's usually so rude to you?"

"He's rude to everyone," Poppy told her.

"But maybe …" she went on uncertainly, "he's changed."

Poppy looked out of the car window into the darkness. Christmas lights were strung in the trees and along the seafront. She thought about how beautiful Brighton looked in the festive season, and suddenly felt very happy that Christmas was on its way.

But something else was making her feel happy too. Poppy was sure that whatever else Ryan did in future, he would never again tell her that dancing was stupid.

Silver Lining

"Ready? Go! *One*, two, three, four, five, six, seven, eight!" called out Miss Johnson. "Straight lines, girls! Get behind Sophie, Debbie! Five, six, seven, eight…"

It was hard to listen to Miss Johnson's instructions and dance at the same time. Poppy and her friends were learning a formation ballroom dance for Miss Johnson's Christmas show. Four boys and eight girls made patterns as they danced, changing position, changing partners and changing rhythm as the music changed. The routine was quite long, so Miss Johnson was teaching it to them bit by bit. But it was still a lot to take in. By the time they'd done the first part six times, Poppy felt dizzy.

"All right, have five minutes' rest," said Miss Johnson, seeing the children were tired. "This is a busy time of year. I'm sure you're involved with lots of things at school."

Poppy sat beside Cora, drinking from her water bottle and thinking about how busy Christmas was. *Cinderella*, her school pantomime, had taken place last week. Poppy hadn't danced in that, but she'd

worked hard teaching dances to the other children. On the last day of term she and the older children would watch the infants' nativity play and join in Christmas songs with the parents afterwards. Then, only two days later, Poppy would be dancing in the Blue Horizon Christmas show. What a lot to do!

"My feet hurt already," said Cora. "Do you think Miss Johnson wants us to rehearse every night this week?"

Poppy nodded. "I don't think your feet are going to get much rest, Cora."

Cora made a face. Then her bright eyes got brighter, and she giggled in the way that always made Poppy herself giggle. "But I *lurve* dancing, so I don't care!"

Neither did Poppy. It never mattered how much work she and the others did, it was always worth it. Knowing a performance went well was the best feeling Poppy knew.

"Let's get back to work!" called Miss Johnson. "I want to have a costume meeting before you go. Now, remember you mustn't cross this line I've taped on the floor."

The twelve formation dancers would be performing in the space left on Miss Johnson's studio floor after the folding rows of seats, which she called her "grandstand", had been set up. Poppy was amazed the first time two men wheeled the grandstand out and let the seats down, transforming the studio into a theatre. She was used to it now, but the children who hadn't been at the Blue Horizon last Christmas had never seen it before.

"What will happen if I *do* cross the line?" Poppy heard Little Tom mutter to Sam.

"You'll fall off the edge of the world," said Sam with a straight face.

"No, *really*, Sam!"

"You'll kick someone sitting in the front row," replied Sam. "That's where the seats will be."

"Concentrate, boys!" called out Miss Johnson.

They began to dance again. They did the routine better, as Poppy had often noticed they did after a break. "Well done," said Miss Johnson. "And now I'll go and get the costumes."

Emma touched Poppy's arm. "What's a costume meeting?" she asked. She had been too shy to ask Miss Johnson.

"It's when we try on the costumes for our dance," explained Poppy.

Emma looked puzzled. "But our mums or dressmakers make our dresses," she said.

This was quite true. Poppy's dresses for tests and competitions were made by a lady called Mrs Heatherington, but for the Christmas show it was different.

"Miss Johnson's got a lot of costumes that have been used before, in other shows," Poppy told Emma. "She'll bring in different sets for us to try on."

"Really? I can't wait!" exclaimed Emma. She even skipped a little, though her feet must have been as tired as Poppy's. "I love trying on costumes!"

Emma wasn't the only one. When Miss Johnson wheeled in a rack of dresses,

catsuits,
trousers,
ties and
waistcoats,
all the children
were excited.

"Wow!" said
Debbie, who, like Emma,
had never seen the costume rack before,
"where do we start?"

"Here," said Miss Johnson. From the rail
she took a dress of the palest blue, with
floats – pieces of light material that floated
when the dancer moved – on the shoulders.
"I thought we might use these, as there's a
whole set. Do you like them, girls?"

Poppy and Emma looked at each other.
Did they like them!

The girls passed the
dresses around until
each of them had one
they thought would
fit. When Poppy held
hers up in front of the
mirror, she found that the
skirt was lined with silver
material. It was so delicate

that a thousand different colours seemed to
shimmer in it. Poppy picked up the hem and
swung the skirt. The lining appeared, then
disappeared, like a shower of silver rain.

"These dresses are *beautiful!*" she said to
Miss Johnson.

The boys had blue shirts and black trousers
with a band of blue and silver material
round their waists. Poppy saw Sophie and

Sam exchange an excited look. Everyone liked the costumes.

"Why not try them on?" suggested Miss Johnson.

The costumes looked great. When the girls and boys lined up in their dance formation, their teacher's face shone. "Lovely!" she exclaimed. She took a small pad of paper and a tin of safety pins from one of the boxes. "Now, take the costumes off and pin your names on them. Your parents will be here to pick you up in a minute."

That evening Poppy couldn't stop talking about the Christmas show. She chattered on and on and whirled round the sitting-room, showing Mum her steps for the part of the dance they'd learned so far.

"Give it a rest, will you, Poppy?" asked Tom, after a while. "I'm trying to watch TV."

He was slumped in the corner of the sofa with his head on his hand. He looked tired, as he often did these days. He had started secondary school this term and was always busy with homework, football and the other thing he liked, such as music – and especially singing.

Poppy sat down in the other corner of the sofa. "I'm so excited!" she said.

"When is your Christmas show anyway?" asked her brother, picking up the TV remote.

"The first Saturday of the holidays at two thirty," Poppy told him happily. "You'll come, won't you?"

Tom started to say something,

then he stopped. A dismayed look came over his face. He turned off the sound on the TV and looked at Poppy. "Did you say the first Saturday of the holidays?" he asked. "The twenty-second of December?"

Poppy nodded.

"But that's when my carol service is!"

Mum looked up from the newspaper. "Oh, my goodness, so it is," she said. "But don't worry, Dad will go to one and I'll go to the other. He always says that's how we split ourselves in half, remember?"

"But, Tom!" said Poppy. "You always come to things I'm in…"

"Except when I've got football practice," he reminded her.

"And I really want to come and hear you sing," she went on.

Tom put the volume up on the TV again, slumping down even further among the cushions. "I know," he said, "but it's no big deal."

Poppy thought it *was* a big deal. Tom had auditioned three times for a solo at the carol service. By next Christmas, his voice would have started breaking. So this would be his only chance to sing the solo first verse of "In the Bleak Midwinter". Just thinking about how beautiful his voice would sound in the huge church made Poppy tingle.

When Tom had gone to do his homework, Poppy squashed into the armchair beside her mum. "Can't we do anything?" she asked.

"What about, love?"

"I'm dancing in the show, but I want to go to Tom's carol service too."

Mum gave kissed the top of her head. "Dad and I can be in two places at once, but *you* can't split yourself in half," she said.

School finished early on the last day of term, after the nativity play and Christmas songs. Mum was busy at the hotel, but Auntie Jill came to hear the children sing and join in the carols. Afterwards she took Poppy's hand and they began to walk up the hill to the Hotel Gemini, their scarves wound tightly against the cold wind.

"Do you think it'll snow?" Poppy asked her aunt.

"The weather forecast said it's too cold for snow," replied Auntie Jill. "But sometimes it's wrong, of course."

"I hope it *doesn't* snow," said Poppy. "I don't want people to get stuck on Saturday going to Miss Johnson's show, or Tom's carol service."

Auntie Jill must have heard the sadness in Poppy's voice. She squeezed Poppy's hand tighter. "You don't mind, do you, that I'm going with Dad to the carol service?" she asked. "Uncle Simon and Mum will come to see you dance."

"No," said Poppy. She knew she couldn't change the arrangement.

"I just wish I could go to the carol service too."

Auntie Jill sighed. "Christmas is always like this. Everything happens at once," she said. "Weren't the little children sweet this afternoon, singing 'Away in a Manger'? That's my favourite carol." And she began to sing it.

Poppy knew her aunt was changing the subject to try and make her feel better. So she joined in the carol, and by the time they'd sung all the verses they were in the warm hotel lobby, pulling off their gloves.

Mum was behind the reception desk. "How did it go?" she asked.

But before they could answer, the glass door swung open and Tom came in. His school had broken up early too. "Did you hear what happened?" he asked breathlessly.

"About the flood?"

"What flood?" asked Mum and Auntie Jill and Poppy together.

Tom put his school bag down. "There's been an accident at the church," he said. "It's all right, no one got hurt. A water pipe burst and the church has been flooded."

"Oh no!" gasped Auntie Jill.

"The school's going to put out an announcement on local radio. They can't possibly have the carol service on Saturday."

"What a shame," said Mum sympathetically.

"Mr McAllister, our music teacher, says they can probably get the hall ready by Sunday evening," said Tom, "so they'll have the carol service then instead of the usual Sunday service."

Poppy began to jump up and down. Although the news about the flood was unfortunate, she couldn't help feeling pleased. "That means I can come to hear you sing on Sunday!" she told her brother. "And you can come and see me dance on Saturday!"

Tom's worried expression turned into a smile. "Wow! That's right!" he said.

"If you want to, I mean," added Poppy.

"Of course I want to," he said. Unwinding his scarf, he picked up his bag and started to climb the stairs. Then he stopped, his hand on the banister rail, and looked back at Poppy. "Every cloud has a silver lining, eh, Poppy?"

Poppy jumped up and down some more. She thought she had never been more proud of her cheerful brother, who never let on when he was upset. And she couldn't wait to hear his voice make *everyone* in the church tingle, flood or no flood.

"A silver lining!" she cried. "Just like my blue dress!"

Doctor Dancing

The next morning Poppy woke up feeling peculiar. When she tried to swallow, her throat was very scratchy. Her head ached, too.

Mum opened the bedroom door, her arms full of clean washing. "Good morning!" she said gaily. "First day of the holidays!"

"Mum, I don't feel well," said Poppy. "My throat hurts."

"Oh dear." Mum looked concerned.

She put down the pile of washing and felt Poppy's forehead. "You might have a fever," she said. "I'd better take your temperature."

She went off to get the thermometer. Poppy lay among the pillows with her eyes closed, feeling a little sorry for herself. Then, all of a sudden, her eyes snapped open and she sat up. She'd remembered something important.

"I can't be ill!" she thought. "I'm dancing in the Christmas show tomorrow, and it's the dress rehearsal today!"

She and her friends had been practising their dances for weeks. Poppy and Zack were in several things together, but she was especially looking forward to doing the formation dance in her beautiful blue and silver dress.

If one of the dancers wasn't there, the dance would be completely spoilt. It would be like a mouth with a front tooth missing!

"Mum!" she called, her voice croaky. She began to get out of bed. "Mum! What about the rehearsal?"

"Shush, now," soothed Mum, coming in with the thermometer. She pressed it across Poppy's forehead.

Mum removed the thermometer and looked at it carefully. Then, to Poppy's surprise, she smiled. "You haven't got a fever," she said. "That's a relief! But you look very pale. Thank goodness there's no school."

"But the show's tomorrow!" protested Poppy. "And Tom's carol service is on Sunday. *And* it's nearly Christmas!"

As she said this, her throat hurt so much and her head ached so badly, and she felt so disappointed, that she began to cry. Tears trickled down her face onto her pyjamas. She held Lucky, her toy puppy, and he got wet too. "It's not fair!" she wailed.

Mum cuddled her, rocking her and stroking her hair. "Calm down, sweetheart," she said.

"But I *have* to dance!" insisted Poppy, hiccupping a little from crying. "I can't let Miss Johnson and the others down."

"Perhaps," said Mum. "Now, I'll get you some medicine, and then you can go back to sleep."

It wasn't long after Poppy had taken two teaspoonfuls of the pink medicine that she was fast asleep. And when she woke up, Auntie Jill was sitting by her bed. "How do you feel?" she asked.

Poppy swallowed. Her throat didn't feel so sore, and her headache had gone. She felt cosy and warm in bed. But the thought of the show pushed everything else out of her mind. "What time is it?" she asked. "I mean, I feel better, thanks. But I've got to go to the dress rehearsal."

Auntie Jill smiled. "The rehearsal's almost over," she told Poppy. "You've been asleep for quite a while. Miss Johnson and the others send their love."

"Oh!" said Poppy, amazed. "But how could they rehearse without me?"

"Miss Johnson danced your part, I expect," said Auntie Jill. "Now, I'll bring you some soup, and we'll have you well in no time."

"Well enough to dance tomorrow afternoon?" asked Poppy anxiously.

"We'll see," said Auntie Jill, and she left the room.

Poppy knew that grown-ups always said "we'll see" when they were probably going to say "no" in the end. She imagined Miss Johnson doing the formation dance with Zack and the others, but the thought didn't make her smile. If Poppy couldn't be there, dancing in her blue and silver costume like all the others, everything would be ruined. She must get better, she just *must*!

Auntie Jill came in with a fresh drink and some soup on a tray, and helped Poppy to sit up in bed. "I'll be back very soon to see how you are," she told her. "And so will Mum when she can get away from the hotel,

and Dad when he gets home from work."

"Where's Tom?" asked Poppy. She didn't want the soup.

"He's gone Christmas shopping, I think," replied her aunt. "Poppy, aren't you hungry?"

Poppy shook her head.

Auntie Jill took her hand. "You're upset about the show, aren't you?" she asked softly.

Poppy nodded miserably. She was afraid that if she spoke she'd cry.

"Well then," said Auntie Jill, "let me tell you about Doctor Dancing."

"Who?" asked Poppy.

"It's not a person," explained Auntie Jill. "It's something I discovered when I was a dancer. My partner and all my friends knew about it too."

"What is it?" asked Poppy, interested.

"Doctor Dancing makes you able to dance even when you don't feel like it," said Auntie Jill. "Of course, if you're really ill, or injured, you can't go on and that's that. But when you've got a cold – like you have – or you're very tired, or sad about something, somehow you forget it when you start to dance."

"So dancing is like medicine, making you better, you mean?" said Poppy.

"That's right," said her aunt. "I remember having awful blisters on my feet the night I won the National Latin American title, but I didn't feel them at all."

"Do you think Doctor Dancing will make me better by tomorrow afternoon?" asked Poppy.

"If you help by having this soup and not worrying," said Auntie Jill.

Poppy finished her soup and snuggled down with her cuddly toy dog Lucky among the pillows, thinking about Doctor Dancing. Did it work just by *imagining* yourself dancing in a blue and silver dress? It seemed to, because she definitely felt better. "I can't wait to start dancing!" she told Lucky.

Mum took Poppy's temperature again the next morning. "Still no fever," she said. "How's your headache?"

"Gone," said Poppy.

"And your sore throat?" asked Mum.

"Gone," said Poppy again.

"What about sniffles?"

"Still here," said Poppy.

Mum laughed. "Better keep this box of tissues near you, then." She looked at Poppy with her head on one side.
"You do look better this morning, I must say."

Poppy didn't mention Doctor Dancing. It was a secret between her and Auntie Jill. "Can I dance this afternoon, then?" she asked.

Mum nodded. "I think so. It's only a mild cold, and you've been such a good girl."

"Awesome!" cried Poppy, and she hugged her.

"But don't give *me* a cold!" said Mum as she hugged Poppy back.

Tom put his head round Poppy's bedroom door. "What's happening?" he asked.

"Mum says I'm well enough to be in the show," Poppy told him happily.

"That's good," he said. "But stay away from me! If I get a cold I won't be able to sing tomorrow."

Tomorrow Tom would be singing a solo in a big church in front of hundreds of people. Poppy wondered if there was a Doctor Singing. "Don't worry," she said, "I promise I won't try to kiss you or anything."

Tom made a face. "You'd better not!" he said, and disappeared.

Mum looked at Poppy with a "boys!" expression. Then she ran a bath for Poppy and helped her get dressed. "You're a very important person today," she told her as she did her hair, "and Tom will be tomorrow. You're both my stars."

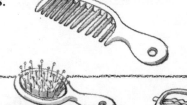

When she got to the Blue Horizon Dance Studio, Poppy was excited. But when she saw the transformation that had taken place there, she felt nervous too. So many people were going to watch her dance!

There were rows of seats around three sides of the dance floor. On the fourth side a curtain hid the area where the children changed. The studio ceiling was covered with twinkling Christmas decorations, and fairy lights were strung like garlands around the walls.

"Hi, Poppy! Are you feeling better?" asked Sophie when she saw Poppy.

"We were worried you wouldn't be able to dance," said Sam, a relieved smile all over his face.

Though everyone was glad that Poppy was there, it didn't make her feel less nervous. The children did their warm-up in a smaller studio while the audience arrived. Dancing made Poppy's nose run, and she had to stop and get a tissue.

"You can't wipe your nose in the middle of a real dance," said Zack.

"Don't worry," Poppy told him, "I won't."

"I'm nervous," admitted Zack, who always was.

"So am I," said Poppy. "More nervous than I usually am, even at competitions. I wonder why."

"It's the formation dance," said Zack. "Too many people to let down."

"Good luck, anyway," encouraged Poppy.

"Thanks, Pop," said Zack. "Good luck."

Poppy was in two things in the first half of the show, a samba routine with Zack, Sophie, Sam, Cora and Luke, and a dance with Miss Johnson's smallest girls. Poppy was supposed to be the queen of the witches, and the little girls her mischievous helpers. They danced in circles around her, wearing black costumes with pointy hats. It was a charming routine, and Poppy hoped no one noticed when her nose started to run, and she had to take a big sniff. She dipped her head so that the brim of her own pointy hat hid her face.

In the interval Poppy felt very tired. She was glad that all she had to do in the second half was the formation dance that ended the show. Mum looked at her carefully as she helped her into the shimmering blue and silver dress. "Are you sure you're OK, love?" she asked.

"Come on, Doctor Dancing," said Poppy to herself. Out loud she said, "Fine. I've only got one more dance to do." Then she sneezed.

"Well," said Mum doubtfully, handing her a tissue, "just make sure you keep warm while you're waiting. Here, put your cardigan on."

Poppy and Zack were to lead the couples out for the formation dance. When Poppy took off her cardigan, there were goose bumps on her arms even though the studio was very warm. Her nerves had come flooding back. She couldn't stop thinking about what Zack had said: "Too many people to let down." And if her nose ran, she had no witch's hat to hide under.

When the music began, Zack held up her hand and they danced onto the floor, the other couples following them and doing exactly what they did. Poppy and Zack got into a ballroom hold and broke away from the line, taking up their position and waiting while everyone else did the same. Poppy smiled at the audience, wishing she could see Mum and Dad, Auntie Jill, Uncle Simon and Tom. But the seats were in darkness, and the spotlights shining in her eyes made it impossible to see anyone. She felt a tickle in her nose, and sniffed.

Then, at that
moment, some sort of
magic took place. Under the spotlight,
with Zack's arm embracing her back and her
hand on his shoulder, Poppy's legs suddenly
seemed to take on a life of their own. Music
and applause filled the room, and the lights
sparkled like diamonds. Poppy's dress
glittered and swirled as she spun, and she
kicked and tripped her way through the steps
without even thinking about her footwork.

She forgot all about the tickle in her nose, and how tired she was. She felt as if she could dance for ever and ever, like the princesses in the story who danced so much that they wore out their shoes every night. As the formation dancers struck their finishing pose and the audience burst into applause, she was sorry it had to end.

"I could do that all over again!" she said to Zack and they bowed and curtseyed.

"I thought you didn't feel well," he said.

"I feel great!" she replied.

And to herself she said, "Thank you, Doctor Dancing!"

Natasha May loves dance of all kinds. When she was a little girl she dreamed of being a dancer, but also wanted to be a writer. "So writing about dancing is the best job in the world," she says. "And my daughter, who is a dancer, keeps me on my toes about the world of dance."

Shelagh McNicholas loves to draw people spinning around and dancing. Her passion began when her daughter, Molly, started baby ballet classes, "and as she perfected her dancing skills we would practise the jive, samba and quickstep all around the house!"